The Art of Cheating Episodes: S1E2

Hangover

EXTENDED AUTHOR'S CUT EDITION

HoLLyRod

COPYRIGHT

Road to Closure
TAOC Prelude
Episode II

April 2012

"You know...the only problem with your little trip down memory lane...is that you're not telling the whole truth HoLLy. And you fucking know it."

Of course the ~~beast~~ wouldn't approve of my reflecting. He never does. Reflection forces you to take a look in the mirror and see the parts that are not so pretty. And I've never done it in this way, so thoroughly.

I never had reason to. And even if I did, time never slowed down long enough for me to take a real step back. Yet and still, deep down, I'm certain that the ~~beast~~ woulda never gave me the luxury...even with time on our side.

Well tonight I've been forced to reflect, before my life truly flashes in front of my eyes at the end of this road. Like I said earlier, I have to at least keep it real with *myself* right now. It's like Dr. Julie always tells me, "*You've gotta acknowledge where you've been to foresee where you may be going Rodney.*"

"It's just me and you in the car right now nigga — which means it's just me," I remind my alter-ego matter-of-factly. *"Who am I lying for? Fuck outta here!"*

I'm sick of his shit. For real this time.

"Nigga you was doing all'at crying and whining about the Curse and the deja vu and how somehow – this shit with Sug is because of the freedom I earned after KeLLy's Revenge!"

"Yeah and?" my voice cracked. *"That Warrensburg sign ain't no coincidence. If it wasn't for* **KeLLy's Revenge***, I woulda never fell for the okie-doke with Sassy. And if it wasn't for Sassy, I woulda never started chasing a dream you never let us stop chasing. All'at shit makes perfect sense to me."*

My eyes reflexively shift focus to the flashing lightning bolts that rip the foggy sky up ahead. It's ten minutes 'til **3am** now. I guess I'm making good timing – considering I'm already past Warrensburg and nearly in Knob Noster, Missouri. Unlike the night of ***KeLLy's Revenge***, the Burg wasn't my destination tonight. I've gotta get back to Saint Louis and, good timing or not, I gotta keep reminding myself that I'm on a tight schedule.

If I drive the limit, I'm three hours away. Somehow though…I have to try to make it in just under *two* hours to catch Sug before it's too late. She has a damn good head start with the way she snuck and left me behind earlier tonight.

Stupid bitch.

The more I think about it, I need to make it in like 90 minutes to realistically have a fighting chance. But I'ma catch this bitch if it's the last thing I do in this world. I just can't let her get the best of me, whether me and the ~~beast~~ see eye-to-eye on her motives or not. I'm not ready to give in to my would-be demise, regardless of how much

I'm in my feelings on this highway. Not tonight. I'll kill this bitch before I let that happen. I will catch her – one way or another. My life depends on it.

"But we ain't gon catch nothing if you don't get off this hoe shit you on HoLLy! It is what it is – why can't we just leave it at that and stay focused??"

"How the fuck am I on hoe shit bro? You saw the Warrensburg sign. The Curse is talking loud and clear – you just don't wanna listen. For once, we need to just be real about what's plain to see."

"That's what I'm saying – you still ain't keeping it real! Why even bring up the Sassy shit if you only telling half the truth about it?"

"Man get the fuck outta here dawg. Everything I said was true. You just hate that I'm putting it all on record and exposing our conflict."

"Take some ownership HoLLy. You're only at conflict with yourself. Put that on record nigga."

Sometimes I wish I could trace my steps and start all the way over. You know – go back to the days before I could actually hear his voice. When my lustful and mischievously dark thoughts were just that – *thoughts*. It was all easier to control back then.

"More lies."

"Whatever nigga."

I've almost learned how to ignore him when he's

vii

slanderous like this. But how do you stop an itch from getting under your skin when that's where it lives? How can I truly drown out the sound of a voice that sounds so much like my own? If there's a such a thing as a voice of reason….my inner ~~beast~~ has always been the opposite.

"Unless I haven't…"

"What is it you keep saying I'm lying about? Humor me."

"Oh nigga, for one — that relapse was a joke! That wuttin' no real 'relapse' into old ways. You talking like that just made you leave my cage unlocked. That's a lie nigga. You never even fucked Sassy's friend Chelle!"

"Well I never said I did fuck Chelle! That's beside the point! Cuz if Chelle didn't ask me for the hooKup with Ricky – you woulda stayed in my ear about it! Like you kept staying in my ear after the relapse, pressuring me to keep pushing limits! You never let me stay on the right path dawg!"

"You coulda prolly still fucked Chelle though," the ~~beast~~ implied with his usual toxic deflection.

"See what I mean bro? You stay on dat bullshit dawg."

"Aww nigga, I'm just talking shit! But thank the cheat gawds the homie Ricky Rhymes took care of Chelle. Cuz I'm just saying. After Sassy, you put me back in the cage like a scary hoe for no reason."

"Forever on bullshit, like I said. And you stayed on bullshit 'til I let yo ass out again. Now look where it got us – speeding on the highway, chasing a bitch. Again. I shoulda never gave you power after all'at shit. I bet that's what the Curse is hinting at."

"Damn you in yo fee fees for real tonight huh HoLLy? Tell me how you really feel then! But stop all the lies though...that ain't a good look."

"Man fuck you, nigga. Truth hurts."

The silence that followed was chilling. He knows I'm right about this. That whole Sassy situation was completely outta bounds. Reckless and sloppy as fuck. The fact that her boyfriend also worked with us just made it all that more fuckin' belligerent. I was lucky that nothing got back to Kells, and the close call had me ready to stop while I was ahead. But the thought of chasing new fantasies had fueled and empowered the beast, and that Sassy shit would ultimately lead to a full-blown relapse later down the line. Damn right I threw the beast back in the cage after Sassy, but eventually his ass just broke free again.

In a world full of lies and lust, sometimes giving in...can be the only way out. But did I truly give in to my innermost desires to break free of the beastly hold it had on *me*...or could it have been the other way around? My brain keeps spinning behind the irony of it all.

The Art of Cheating is real...as real as ***The Son's Curse*** I live with. Pops told me when I first hit puberty how the *Curse* works – he said that '*no matter what you do to them, women will love you blindly and you won't be able to get rid of certain ones forever*'. He told me the spirits of certain love flames could even reappear in others, sometimes years after the relationship had ended. In my younger days, I was skeptical. The shit sounded like another one of Pops' creative jokes. By the time I was in college, I was forced to take heed.

It was my college years where the Curse showed me how serious my dad was. For lack of a less corny way to put it – I couldn't beat the ladies off me with my Kappa kane. It didn't help that I was curiously young, dumb, and full of cum. And so, to manage and minimize any potential drama that could come along with the side effects of the Curse, I started to learn and practice the principles of this thing called *The Art of Cheating*.

"Half-truths never hurt at all HoLLy. Remember that rule? You found the Art long before I had a voice, and you couldn't handle it. You needed me."

He's right about that – with his petty ass. In the beginning, there was no ~~beast~~. I tapped into the ability to creep with multiple women on the fly mostly, but also mostly on my own. The thrill and rush of not getting caught up started to make me feel invincible. The better I got, the more I tried to get away with it. That greed strengthened this brewing force of nature in my inner spirit and thus the belligerent whispers of the ~~beast~~ were born.

"Ok, but how the fuck did I need you though? Yea, I know the rules nigga – and so do you. 'We tell no lies…only half-truths'. No lies, remember? You outta line for even going there right now."

"Ok, you right. That's my bad on the L word. No lies."

"Yeah, tighten up nigga. We gotta stay focused, remember?"

"Aight — I just said I ain't gon say the L-word again. I'm just saying — like you said — it's just me and you right now. You claim it's time to be honest about everythin..."

"Cuz it is. This time we went too far."

"Ok, even if that's the case — which you know damn well I don't believe. But if that's the case...what happened to being completely honest nigga? Why you still telling half-truths...to yourself?"

"What's the whole truth nigga?"

"The whole truth is — you needed me. You 'wanted' to chase those fantasies...you 'wanted' to pursue those heartless thoughts. But you needed me for the power to push you. You needed me...to care less."

I like to think that every human has an inner beast. The lustful energy and carefree boldness that is mine was hard not to give in to. But did I actually *need* to give it this much control? I doubt it.

I found *The Art of Cheating*, on my own, as a way to manage the curse of being a natural-born ladies' man. But managing the belligerence of my inner beast has been just as much of a job in itself. That's where the conflict comes in. I know the audacity of my darkest thoughts is wrong, but *The Art* helps me paint with disappearing ink. That's a lot for any nigga to try to juggle all at once.

"That don't change the fact that you needed me cuz you couldn't handle The Art on your own. When you gon speak to the fact that you was always sloppy without me?"

"*Aww come on dawg – I thought we wuttin' doing the L-word? Who telling half-truths now?*"

"*Keep it a hunnid HoLLy! You can't think of a time prior to KeLLy's Revenge – where you didn't need me to do what you do effectively. You said we got time, right? Don't worry, I'll wait.*"

"*Nigga please! I practiced* **The Art** *for years before* **KeLLy's Revenge!!!**"

"*Then speaking on just one time should be an easy challenge. Get out ya lil voice recorder. I'm listening HoLLyRod...*

"*Nigga it ain't like we gotta think that hard! I* **been** *surgical with* **The Art** *dawg – you know that's real talk. Hell…I was moving like a fuckin' Jedi the whole summer* **right** *before* **KeLLy's Revenge!** *Must I remind you about the* **Hangover** *episode???*"

*　　*　　*　　*　　*

...to be continued in TAOC Episodes S1E2

Road to Closure: Episode II

Have you ever seen a picture or a portrait —
full of beautiful color and intricate detail, so
complex and deep, and exploding with pure
artistry???? Give it but a glance and you'll never
appreciate the true brilliance behind it.
Yet…stare at it for too long….and you'll
become consumed by its mystique and engrossed
to near obsession.

Cheating is a work of art.

This…

…is the masterpiece that I've always liked to
call…

The Art of Cheating

1

July 2003
9:21am

Last night was mad real. My breath reeked of dry gin, and my clothes were stained with vomit of whatever had been my last meal. My head was pounding, heart thumping as I laid still. Eyes closed shut.

It had to be almost midday by now, I felt like I had been lying face down forever. My keys were in the right pocket of my khaki shorts, pressing hard against my thigh. I knew my leg had to be bruised, I could feel it throbbing with irritation.

Sounds of *India Arie's* first album *'Acoustic Soul'* poured out the speakers a few feet to my right. Damn, that shit seemed too loud. I could hear KeLLy's voice to my right, talking even louder above the music, "Girl that's what I asked when they carried him in! Did somebody put something in his drink? But they just kept saying *'naw, that ain't how it went down.'*"

Another voice chimes in, "Yeah cuz you know that happened to my friend *Teresa*! Girl, she couldn't remember shit! Ok?!? I thought the bitch was in a coma."

The next voice I recognize as KeLLy's cousin, Renée, "Oh that's right, I forgot all about that – at *Jerry's* lil party

1

or whatever! Yeah see you gotta be careful, that's why I don't be drinking for real when we go out!

"Tilt ya head this way, *Ana*," KeLLy says. "Hell, I don't know – but his ass been laying there in the middle of the floor for hours."

"Girl shut up!" Renée squeals. "Why they didn't carry him to the bedroom?!?!"

KeLLy laughs, but I can tell she doesn't think any of it is funny. "They barely carried him through that front door, it was only Ricky and Malone. Y'all know how little *Malone* is."

Ana, KeLLy's other cousin who is apparently getting her hair braided, then exclaims, "Girl I cannot see Lil Malone tryna carry somebody!"

"Now which one is Malone?" Renée asks. "You know I get all his frat brothers mixed up – I don't know how you deal with that. Better than me, that's the truth."

"You learn names after a while girl, hush up. Malone is the little short, crazy acting one. Always act like he done drank a *Red Bull*. Hyper n'shit," Kells explains.

Renée catches on, as her memory is jolted, "Right ok, I think I know which one you talking about. Now who else was helping him? Cuz you sholl right – Malone little ass ain't bout to be carrying nobody. Not even Rodney's boney ass!"

KeLLy went on to explain to her two cousins again how I ended up in the middle of the living room floor and hadn't budged much since. The important parts of it I could remember vividly, as I heard KeLLy tell the story again for what seemed like the 50th time...

*   *   *   *   *

6:19am

"I'm coming – *hold on* – damn!!!" KeLLy screamed in frustration as **Ricky** beat on the front door like the police. Or maybe it was my other frat brother **Malone** beating on the door while Ricky held my nearly limp body up on his shoulder. I honestly can't remember who was doing the holding and who was doing the knocking. I can say, for sure though, that I distinctively remember the anger and irritation on the other side of the door.

"Nuuupe she bout ta bee maaad at yaalll," my voice was hoarse, and words slurred.

"Nigga she bout to be mad at *yo* drunk ass, that's *yo* girl fool," Ricky chuckled.

My knees buckled as I struggled to stand up straight, and my eyes were low – hurting from the sun shining down directly on the door stoop. My back was sore as shit and it seemed like Kells was taking forever to open the

3

door. She always slept naked though, so more than likely she was trying to get decent.

It was the summer of 2003. KeLLy and I had been living together off campus since last semester. She was going to be a senior the upcoming fall, and I had decided to enroll in grad classes and moved back to the Burg.

Big mistake. A recent college grad such as myself still had a lot of partying to get outta my system – and the Burg was just the right place to do it.

The *Ques* had a probate show the night before – a party and after-party followed. The party after the *after-party* was at Malone's crib – and he and Ricky were just now dropping me off at home as the dawn of the day hit. Like I said…last night was mad real.

"Come on bro," Ricky nodded at Malone as they helped me up on the door stoop and toward the doorway. Then at me, "Rod watch out nigga! Do NOT get that throw-up on me Nupe!"

The stench from the bottom of my shirt was still fresh, and I tried to lean away from Ricky to avoid touching. My right knee was in excruciating pain, so I barely made it.

At that point, the door swung open furiously and KeLLy stood there in a pink robe, arms folded.

"Ok now y'all, it is *6:30* in the mutha-freakin' *morning* – I cannot *WAIT* to hear this shit!!!" she yelled. Then, without budging...and more calmly, "Go on, I'm listening..."

* * * * *

2

Ricky didn't hesitate and spoke first.

"KeLLy, yes we apologize for banging on your door like the police at 6 in the morning...but can we please bring him in? This little nigga is heavier than he looks," he pleaded, regaining his composure as my body slumped downward.

KeLLy's scowl was just as piercing through squinted eyes. Yet, she stepped backwards to make room for us.

Ricky & Malone weren't on the same pace as they struggled to pull me past the white-colored door and into the house. As soon as they were a few steps into the open space living room, Ricky kneeled down to lower me to the floor, but Malone didn't follow suit. They nearly dropped me face first – but Ricky's reflexes were on point, as he put his hand out to the floor to catch himself, and my upper torso fell against his shoulder. Malone's delayed reaction would have given any onlooker cause to argue who was more intoxicated – him or me. He finally caught on and took a knee.

"You don't wanna take him to the room or

7

something?" Malone asks Ricky.

"Fuck that, lay this guy right here," Ricky responds with certainty. "He cool right the fuck here."

"*RODNEY!!!*" KeLLy yells in my ear as a fall to the hard floor. "What the hell y'all?"

Malone laughs, "Rod got too gone last night!!!"

"Bro this shit ain't even funny," Ricky tries to check him, noticing Kells' irritation.

"This guy...wow," she rolls her eyes. "Ricky, what the hell is going on?"

Ricky softens his tone as he spits it out, "Yeah he got too fucked up last night, mixing light & dark. But real shit, we *all* got fucked up. Rod just got real ***belligerent*** – well should I say, *more* belligerent than usual."

"I told him not to mix the dark!" Malone keeps chuckling.

My lady was even more agitated now than before. "*Ok* he got drunk, y'all got effed up – hell we all been pissy drunk before," she snaps. "But come on now – the damn *birds* are outside chirping n'shit!!!"

"Yea, real spit...we didn't even know he was still at the house," Ricky continues. "Well lemme speak for *myself* – I know *I* thought he was already back home, we just found him in the laundry room about a half hour ago."

KeLLy joins Malone in the laughter, as she tries to keep her top from blowing. "Oh....y'all just *'found'* him? In the laundry room."

Malone keeps giggling along with her, oblivious to the fact that KeLLy didn't really find any humor in this. Ricky kept explaining things from his point of view:

*After the Que probate, we all went to the party downtown. Since the Nupes and Ques historically were close friends, the bar gave us free well drinks. Mostly gin & tonic for Rod, but vodka was in the air too. Long story short – the party ended early after two fights, and then the Ques had an after-party at their house everybody slid to. The Ques had a liter of **Hennessy** at the house and started passing shots out, apparently Rod took a bunch of shots to the head. After a while, folks started complaining about how hot the basement was (no AC on the lower level) and so the Nupes suggested we move the party to Malone's crib on the west side. After only a couple people showed up to Malone's, Ricky and Rod rode to get some **Taco Bell** while Malone stayed behind in case more folks showed....*

"Errbody was too gone!!" Malone steps in, still laughing. "Turned it on in yo!"

Ricky bites his lip, side-eyeing our frat brother. "So yeah, Rod eats his food too fast in the car, and threw up once we got back to the house," he tells my girl.

KeLLy bends down to try to turn me over on my side, either to look at my shirt or help me take it off. I groaned in agony, reaching for my right knee.

"Boy I'm trying to get this nasty ass shirt off! Fine,

9

keep it on!" she screams. "So what the hell happened to his *knee*?!?!?!"

Ricky replies, "Oh yeah – the nigga slipped walking up the steps when we was leaving the Ques'...tweaked his shit again. Almost forgot about that."

That causes KeLLy to throw her hands up in frustration and defeat. I can tell she's sick of our shit.

"I helped him to the bathroom after he threw up and then I left," Ricky stays focused.

"You *left*?" KeLLy echoes in disbelief.

"Yeah, I mean – I ain't gon front, I had some action. So, I shook. Nobody showed up to Malone's, so it was time to turn it in. Malone said *he* was gon take Rod home, I took off. I don't know what happened but when I pulled back up, this guy Malone was knocked out on the couch. I thought Rod was at home until I got ready to wash my clothes n'shit."

"I was out after you left, that nigga kept throwing up!" Malone can't wipe the smile off his face, continuing to make matters worse.

"Shut up nigga!" Ricky has had enough. "I'm just saying – KeLLy I'm *saying* – I don't know what happened after *I* left, and I thought he was gone. I almost fell over this fool laid out in the doorway to the laundry room."

"I mean did somebody put something in his *drink*?!?!?!

What the fuck Ricky?!?!" KeLLy wonders.

"Naw, I'm not gon say that. I mean the nigga just mixed that gin with that Henn ya dig?" Ricky says with conviction.

Malone starts rambling, talking shit, "Too gone! Rod know he can't handle that, I told him! I tried to tell him, 'Rod – don't do it! Don't be no fool!'"

"Bro! Chill out!" Ricky yells at him, completely out of patience.

"This don't even make no good damn sense!" KeLLy declares. "Rodney, you too damn old to be drinking like that!!!"

"I mean he gon be ok, he just need to sleep it off," Ricky reassures her, trying to ease the tension. "Like I said, once I found him on the floor – I woke this nigga up and we brought him home. I figured you was worried...or ready to kill this nigga ya dig?"

"Naw I was 'bout to just find me a new roommate, that's all," KeLLy says, almost sounding serious. "Y'all better be lucky *y'all* found him, that's all I'ma say. You get on my damn *nerves* Rodney!"

"Come on Rick, let's carry him to the room," Malone kneels down to my side.

"Naw leave his ass *right* there," KeLLy stops him. "He can lay right the 'eff there 'til he sober up."

"Yeah....naw bro, come on – let's get out dey way," Ricky grabs Malone by the arm. And then to KeLLy, "For real, again – sorry for waking you up this early. Shit I'm sleepy too, niggas ain't had no sleep. We gon go ahead and get outta here..."

"Ok, well thanks – that's fine. I had to get up in a lil bit anyway cause I gotta braid my little cousin's hair in a couple of hours," she says. "So thanks Ricky."

Malone started to say something else, but Ricky pulled him by his arm towards the entrance and they hurried away, KeLLy slamming the door behind them.

That made my head throb, and suddenly I felt real thirsty. I called out to Kells for some water. But needless to say, my throat stayed dry.

"Leave me alone, don't say nothing to me nigga!" she warns.

A long silence followed, and I could hear Kells in the bedroom moving around. Before I realized it, I was out cold on the floor.

9:07am

I woke up to the doorbell ringing repeatedly, and KeLLy stepping over me to get to the door.

Her cousin Ana walked in first, "Now what the *HELL*

12

happened here???"

"Girl! This nigga!" KeLLy smacks her lips. "You got ya hair? Is Renée with you?"

Ana steps over my drunken body before she responds, "Yeah here she come, girl. What this dog ass nigga done did now?"

*   *   *   *   *

3

"So did you check his pockets? I know I'd be all in my man's pockets...*fuck* that!" Renée wants more details.

KeLLy replies quickly, "Girl I'm not 'bout to be all in his pockets, he got that nasty ass shirt he done threw up on! Hellll naaaaw!"

"See that's gross!" Ana is disgusted. "Ewww...uhn uhn...damn shame."

"I ain't bout to go through that boy's pockets," Kells reiterates. "Let his drunk ass sleep."

"KeLLy, you don't wanna turn that music down?" Renée asks, trying to be considerate. "It might be too loud."

"I hope it *is*, dammit!" Kells admits unapologetically.

"So what did y'all do last night?" Ana asks her, in an attempt to lighten the mood. "Did you go out with *Danni* and 'nem?

"Naw girl, I gotta study for this stupid quiz in my summer class. Danni and 'nem stepped out but my black

15

ass was right here on this couch. They said the probate was cool, but they left the party early. I guess some of the football players was down there fighting."

"Again?!?!" Ana is shocked, but I don't know why. "Wasn't they fighting at the last party we drove down for?"

"Girl yes," KeLLy confirms. "It's something wrong with them niggas."

Kells and her kinfolk continued catching up and having girl talk. As I laid on the floor in the middle of the fire, last night was starting to flash in my head in bits and pieces...

* * * * *

10:52pm

The **Ques** had brought out their new pledge line on campus, behind the football stadium. Summer lines were rare, but the Ques had just been reinstated back on the yard the spring semester before. The show was packed, at least for a summer show. Most of the regular students were home for the break, but there was still a good size crowd.

Ricky, Malone, and I made up 3 of the 6 Nupes that

were still in town for the summer. We were already drinking before the probate, and I had my signature *Sunny D* orange drink bottle (spiked strongly with *Seagram's Gin*) in hand during the show. I was definitely on one.

1:09am

The party downtown was where it got crazy. One of the Ques worked as a part time DJ at *The Star Bar* so we all got in free of charge. That also came along with the free well drinks, and I must have had about 7 drinks in about two and a half hours. Good thing I wasn't driving.

This was before my driving days. See most of my life, I was a self-proclaimed '*rider*'. Muhfuckaz from my neighborhood didn't get new cars for graduating HS or college, so I got used to riding shotgun with one of my crew. Wait, now that I think about it, I rarely rode up front. I was always the '*little nigga*' and so at times it made more sense for me to be in the back seat. I never, ever even volunteered to drive – and constantly used the fact that I didn't have a license as my logical excuse whenever I got suggested as a designated driver. Up until the previous summer, that worked. However, KeLLy had made me go get a license once I graduated. Still, I had no car of my own by the summer of '03, and rarely would be the designated driver.

Designated drivers back in these days *really* meant that the one who was *least* drunk had to drive. Malone could *never* handle liquor, so Ricky became that guy on this night by default. He was driving Malone's whip, and I was riding shotgun since Malone was the youngest Nupe. On the ride from downtown to the Ques' house, my head started to spin, and I laid my face against the window.

"You cool bro?" Ricky asked me from behind the wheel. "You want me to drop you off at the crib?"

"Naaaw bro, fuck that," I shoot back. "I'm good, less go."

"Nigga you thew!" Ricky suspects. "You 'bout to start hurling!"

Triggered at the thought of me throwing up in his ride, Malone starts panicking in the backseat, "Pull over yo! Right up here!"

"Naw bruhs, I'm straight – fa real!" I sit up, straightening myself out. "Malone shut yo asss up nigga! You don't e'en kno what planet we on rite now boy..."

Ricky busts out laughing, "Both you niggas done! Y'all lightweights!"

"Aye bro what happened with that one little **Zeta** chick you was rapping with in the corner?" I turn to my left, grinning mischievously.

Ricky's energy switches up as he replies excitedly, "She said she going to the after-party! I'm all on top of that! But dig *this* – her little friend she was with said she wanna see wassup with *Malone*."

I can barely contain my reaction, "*Get* the fuck outta

he..."

"I fuck nothing but dyme pieces yo!" Malone cries out matter-of-factly.

Ricky and I burst into hysterical laughter at our brother, anticipating yet another one of his classic rants about how all the chicks he fucks with are 10's. These same chicks we never see.

"These hoes out here man...yo. Who?! *I'm* out here," Malone keeps rambling on indistinctively.

"Bro what the *fuck* are you talking about?!?" I'm howling. "Are you gon get on her friend or what? Cuz I'm willing to *bet* you babysitting tonight nigga!"

"Dig that! I'll take that bet too," Ricky co-signs.

Malone gets charged up and starts going off about absolutely nothing. "Maaaaaan please! Y'all niggaz – *who?!?!* If she ain't a dyme, I pay her no mind. She can choose me or *lose* me!!"

"He's gone!" I declare. This nigga ain't making no sense.

"Bro you know Malone ain't getting no pussy. Come on bro," Ricky teases.

"I fucks *dymes* nigga!" Malone repeats himself again, demanding acknowledgement.

"What the friend look like?" I ask Ricky, disregarding Malone's outbursts. "I ain't really get a look at the bitch."

Ricky keeps poking, "Oh she ain't no *dyme*! Naw...not near."

"Naw I'm saying – is she *fuckable*?" I'm wondering.

"Very," Ricky confirms. "But again, you know *Malone* ain't bout to..."

"Right, I already know. This nigga ain't had no pussy since he went over," I point out jokingly.

"Yeah *right*, I fucks more than you!" Malone shouts in my left ear from the backseat. I'm clearly under his skin now.

"Don't do this bro," I warn him to tread carefully.

Malone takes another sip from his beer can and goes, "Aye Rick go head and drop Rod off! You know he gotta get home to his *girl* now."

"Nigga I got a girl at the crib and I *still* get mo' pussy than you nigga – stop the madness!" I spew defensively.

Ricky just laughed as he circled the block looking for a parking space. The whole street was lined with cars and the three-story Que house looked just as packed as a club. There was scattered ass everywhere, as chicks were walking in the street from their cars to the house.

"Shit I know I'm 'bout to grab me a lil something – I don't know about *you* niggas!" Ricky announced his plans.

"Nigga I'll bet Malone don't get no pussy tonight if it get *handed* to him!" I said with a devilish undertone.

"Bet something!" Malone doesn't back down.

"How much you wanna lose nigga?!?!" I pressed the issue.

Ricky tries to intervene, realizing where this is going. "Rod don't bet this guy," he pleads with me.

"Bet $20!" Malone throws the wager on the table.

With no hesitation, I scream, *"Bet!!!!"*

And with that, it was on. The rest of the night was set to be pure entertainment for me.

I thought to myself, *'I'ma get fucked up, watch Malone dig a hole and bury himself. My spot is walking distance from the Ques' and I can get me a nice quick one off with KeLLy when I crash.'*

Looking at the time on my Motorola flip phone changed that last thought – it was already **1:15am**. As Ricky finally found a parking spot a block from the house, I realized Kells might already be knocked out by the time I call it a night.

"Nigga I bet *you* don't get no pussy!" Malone doubles down, shifting the focus back to myself.

"Bro come on, you know I got pussy at home," I told him. "This is about you, not me. I ain't seen you get no pussy in two years nigga! Look at all these hoes that came out tonight. Show me something!"

"Aye fuck all'at...spark that L before we go in," Ricky started fumbling around in the ashtray.

"We got 20 on you getting some pussy or what, yo?" I asked Malone to confirm our wager.

"We already bet," he mumbled.

I picked up the tightly rolled Swisher blunt from the ashtray and took the lighter from Ricky, putting flame to the chronic. Smoke filled the car with all the windows rolled up.

We sat in silence for a few minutes until we were interrupted by two knocks on the driver window. The Zeta chick Ricky was plotting on had parked damn near right next to us, with the friend who was crushing on Malone right alongside her.

"Can we smoke with y'all?"

Oh. Shit.

*　　*　　*　　*　　*

S1E2: Hangover

4

1:24am

Aight so...here's the scene. There's now 5 of us –
parked in a white Grand Prix a block away from the after-
party, passing two blunts around. Straight hotbox. The
Zeta, **Tammy**, was a redbone thick mama from Kansas
City. I played it smooth and let her get up front with Ricky
and I hopped in the back next to Malone. On Malone's
other side sat Tammy's friend – **Mona**.

Mona didn't go to school there but was born and
raised about 30 miles east of the Burg. She didn't smoke
and she didn't talk much. Malone was just as silent all of a
sudden.

"Damn young Nupe, you done got shy on us now that
they in here?" I try breaking the ice.

"What is this guy talking about? I'm chilling," Malone
says, convincing himself more than us.

My response is full of sarcasm, "I know."

Ricky and Tammy were whispering to each other by
now in between turns. I was at the perfect high so I
decided to get out the car...almost feeling like a 5th wheel.

25

I mean – technically I was. I wuttin' fucked up about it by any means though, I was just out kicking it like college kids do.

I made my way up the street towards the party, where there was a group of AKAs standing out in the back chanting. One of KeLLy's friends from high school, *Danni*, who'd just crossed last semester, was out there leading the pack. A couple of Ques and some Deltas were off to the side, laughing in drunken fun. When one of the older Ques, *Jay*, seen me walking up, his eyes widened.

"Oh there that nigga is! Smooth ass Kappa ass nigga! I see you boa!!!" Jay started yelling.

"My nigga Jay," I laughed. "I'm just tryna be like you, bro!"

We dapped up, and Jay told one of his neos to grab a shot glass – insisting that I take a shot of *Henn* with him. I tried to decline, telling him I was on white liquor downtown, but Jay started talking shit about Ques pledging harder than Kappas and so I agreed to take one shot.

Three shots later, Jay had me in the basement shooting dice in the corner. The basement was packed...and stuffy. This is where it all went down – the smoke room, the gambling, freaky dances on the wall, the grinding on the couch. Back when the Kappas had a house on campus, we called this area of the party the VIP section.

I stayed down in the basement with Jay until he saw

one of his jump-offs and walked away. I started to move towards the stairs but there was this chick bent over, bouncing her ass in front of me. I tried to go around her, but she twirled to the side and got right in my path. In the split second I paused to react, she had her cheeks pressed up against me, ass barely covered up in her jean shorts.

Dammit. By now I was in a zone, and this was NOT what I needed at the moment. I could feel myself growing below almost instantly. I'm sure she could too, as her bounce turned to a slower grind and she pressed her back into my chest. Instinctively, I pulled her in closer by her waist and started to match her rhythm. Even with it being prior to the day my ~~beast~~ developed a voice, this wasn't good.

2:34am

Four songs later...and *Miss Fat Ass* has backed it up to the arm of the couch on the wall, with me in between. There's four people on the couch, two chicks who are way too cuddled up for it to be so hot in here...and then some other dude is caked up with a bitch on the opposite end. Miss Fat Ass is grinding so hard against me, I damn near fall over the two cuddled-up chicks. One of 'em puts her hand on my back to stop the fall, and I regain my balance. Somewhat at least. Miss Fat Ass then stands up straight and turns around.

"Don't go nowhere," she says. "I gotta go get some air."

27

"Shit, I need some air too. I'm following you."

She smiles and heads towards the stairs, me following closely behind her. We moving real slowly – like I said the basement was crowded – and she's squeezing my hand with hers tightly. My dick starts jumping in my khaki shorts. Right before we get to the stairway, I casually take her hand and put it on my stiffness. The squeezing doesn't stop one bit.

We reach the stairs, and she takes a step upwards, hand still on my crotch. I put my left arm around her waist to stay close. The task is awkward as we walk up the stairs and I struggle to keep my balance.

I gotta weigh in on this situation.

Miss Fat Ass is wearing some cut-off jean shorts – daisy dukes if you will – and her ass cheeks are hanging out. Her halter top is damp with sweat, nipples on point.

I ain't know if she went to school here – since I graduated a year ago, I'm only recently back in town and not officially enrolled for grad school just yet. Faces I don't recognize are just that, and for all I know this bitch could either be a student or just in town on a road trip. I don't know who she knows, so the whole scenario is dangerous as fuck.

But I need to fuck this chick, that's all I can think to myself. I got the strongest urge to take this bitch outside and get it in somewhere, and drunken lustful urges usually get the best of me at this hour.

I need to get Miss Fat Ass outside. The night is still young.

*   *   *   *   *

5

2:47am

We halfway up the stairs now. We've stopped moving, as we stand to the right to let some people walk back down. This is both good and bad.

It's good because now I can stand on the same step as Miss Fat Ass as she continues to rub my dick through my shorts. I'm cuffing her right cheek with my right hand, and I'm inches away from her pussy. You know how you start feeling that warmer area? Feels like the pussy is just blowing heat out like an oven.

On the other hand, heat is almost the last thing I need in my life at this very moment, and we need to keep moving cuz it's hot as fuck in this stairway. There's a whole slew of folks trying to make their way down into the overcrowded basement area, where there's no AC or ventilation. The one ceiling fan and two floor units they got down there ain't cutting it. My wife-beater underneath my *Nautica* polo was drenched with sweat, and I needed some fresh air quick, but we was at a standstill on this endless journey up the stairs.

That makes the situation bad, because not only is it impossible to keep track of how many eyes may be watching, I also hadn't seen the bruhs in way too long. Even though I was in good company at the Ques' house, Nupes had a responsibility and oath to stay close to each other in public crowded situations – in case anything ever went down. I needed to find Ricky and Malone, and at least sync our whereabouts.

Miss Fat Ass leans her head back on her right shoulder, "What's yo name?"

"Rod," I breathe hard in her ear.

"Rod," she repeats. "Don't be shy now. Go 'head..."

Even with all the thoughts running through my head in the midst of the humid chaos, I know exactly what she means and my hand crawls to the left...fingers reaching under her shorts to find her bare kitty. It's creamy wet as I touch it, and she moves closer as I stick my index finger in. It's so fucking warm inside.

Biting my lip with lust, I whisper, "Damn...aww yeah???"

She's grinding her hips against me as I play with her pussy, with her right hand reaching back to grip my **wooD**. She starts to unzip my shorts. Sweat is dripping down my face at this point, and my breathing is speeding up. I need to fuck this chick...that's all I keep thinking.

This is going on for about as long as the length of a *Lil Jon* verse, which is more than likely what was playing at the time. But it felt like it was a *LOT* longer...me standing in the middle of the stairs, finger-fucking this chick while she gives me a hand job. When you drunk and high...everything moves slower...

The pathway finally cleared out, and I could see the doorway to the kitchen up ahead. The three or four people ahead of Miss Fat Ass start to move forward, and I pull my finger out her snatch so she, too, can move forward. As she takes a step, a few more people come in the house through the back door, which directly faces the stairway into the basement. A couple of young cats I didn't recognize...and then a couple of *AKAs* walked in behind them. They gather at the top of the stairs, and I take another step behind Miss Fat Ass.

One of the AKA's shouts out in a loud and high-pitched voice, "Y'all, where **Danni** go?!?!?"

Not two seconds later, I hear Danni's voice, "I'm right here, bitch." I've heard that voice talking to KeLLy enough over the last year to recognize it from anywhere, even in my intoxication.

Panicking, I moved Miss Fat Ass's hand away from my dick and tried to take a step backwards. But remember – everything moves slower when you fucked up – and the stair didn't meet my right foot when I expected it to. I lost balance and my weight came down unevenly on my right knee, causing it to pop out of place. The next thing I know...I'm falling face first towards the stairs...and trying to brace myself with one hand.

Ironically, before my face hits a stair or Miss Fat

Ass's ankle, somebody from behind catches me and I hear another familiar voice, *"Whoa, you cool Nupe?"*

It's Malone. I have no idea where he came from and I ain't even know he was in the basement. But boy was I happy as fuck to see this retarded muhfucka. Malone puts his hand in my armpit and helps me limp up the remainder of the stairs, stopping near the wide-open back door. My face is cringing, expressing my pain. Malone stands next to me and I see Miss Fat Ass standing in the doorway outside the house. I'm almost positive she's waiting on me.

This ain't the first time my knee has popped out of place. It's an old injury from when I was in high school – fucked it up playing basketball and it ain't been the same since. If I ever turn too suddenly, or my weight comes down unbalanced, it never fails. Sometimes it's bad, other times it's really bad. If it pops back in place, at worst I can have some swelling and pain for a few days. When it doesn't pop back in place, I can't even stand up...and the pain lasts for weeks.

Luckily it popped back in place almost immediately this time.

Malone has the ugliest smile on his face, "You good fool? Too much of that juice!"

I'm looking down, grabbing my knee. "Fuck you, nigga," I shoot back.

I suddenly feel a hand on my left shoulder and then

Danni's voice followed up with, *"Rodney...what the hell?!?!"*

Shit.

＊　　＊　　＊　　＊　　＊

11:48am

There's a lot to remember from that point, and it's still all slowly coming back in flashes.

The doorbell is ringing again...and I can hear a bunch of females outside our door. KeLLy gets up to answer it, stepping over my legs, and I turn my head to the other side, eyes cracked open slightly. I don't want to get up from the floor just yet, even though my throat is dry as hell. I ain't even sure if I would make it – the bedroom seemed like a mile away.

Ana is sitting on the floor in front of the couch, hair half-braided with micros. Renée is directly across from me, but on the computer so she's facing the other way. The music is still blasting *India Arie's* voice, and I'm 'bout tired of hearing this shit. Three more chicks come walking in behind KeLLy.

Wow this is turning into a regular fuckin 'Waiting to Exhale' meet around this muhfucka!!! Can I get some peace and quiet around here while I'm tryna recall the greatness from last

35

night??? Kells on some bullshit right now, but shit I ain't bout to get up and protest. I ain't no fool.

I turn my head back to the other side, now facing the wall again.

"Did y'all get the *Bacardi*?" KeLLy asks. "Yasss girl!!!! Please proceed to the kitchen and put that in the freezer, please."

Footsteps walk past me. "Is that *Rodney*?" an unfamiliar voice asks.

Renée speaks up, "Girl yeah with his sorry *drunk* ass...can't even make it to the room. He been sleep since we got here."

Then Kells adds, "Y'all, excuse my *mess* on the floor. I didn't have time to clean it up this morning."

Ouch.

The next voice is familiar to my ears whether intoxicated or in the middle of the biggest **hangover** of my young life...

"Naw **Isha**, we need some cups and ice, bitch! Let's open that bottle *right now!!*" Danni shouts with her usual ratchet energy. "KeLLy – girl!!!! Lemme tell you about *YO* man…last night!"

OUCH MUTHAFUCKIN' OUCH!!!!!

    *   *   *   *   *

6

11:52am

My heart skips a beat.

Then another.

Then still another......

It feels like hours pass before someone else speaks...and the next voice is KeLLy's other friend since high school, *Isha*, hollering from the kitchen, "Kel, y'all got some plastic cups?"

"Yeah, here I come, girl," KeLLy replies. "Hold that thought, Danni!"

"Y'all went out last night, Danielle?" Renée asks Danni as Kells walks out the room.

"Girl y'all shoulda came down last night, it was crazy!" Danni tells the crew.

Danni, Isha, and KeLLy have been homegirls for ages. And by ages, I mean that they all actually met in elementary school. So, I'm lying in the middle of the floor, surrounded by two of Kells' closest cousins, two of her closest *childhood friends*, and some other unknown chick...about to hear them talk about what they saw last night. On top of that, the most crucial variable in all of this centered around the relationship I had with Danni. *We hated each other.* She never approved of me with KeLLy, and I couldn't stand her hating ass. This would be the prime opportunity for Danni to start some madness between me and her bff...

Shit just got REAL!!!!

*　　*　　*　　*　　*

3:03am

Hand on my shoulder, Danni had a smirk on her face that I could just spit at.

"Rodney, are you cool? She asks.

"Fuck you Danni," I speak sharply. "Get away from me..."

"Nupe, you want some of this Que punch?" Malone steps in.

He walked off without me answering and left me standing there with Danni.

Thanks again for having my back, Malone.

"You ok Rodney?" Danni's tone switches up. "I thought I saw you *bust* ya ass..."

I was still holding my knee. Danni was now standing to my right, and the door to the back yard was ahead and to my left. From the view I had of the door, I couldn't tell if Miss Fat Ass was still standing there.

"I'm cool, Danni. Why the fuck you acting like you care though?"

"Oh nigga I *don't*," she reminds me. "I'm just making sure you ain't doing nothing you ain't *supposed* to be doing...wit ya dog ass!! Where my girl at anyway?"

"Stay out my bidness homie – I'm a grown ass man!" I turn my nose up.

"Yeah well, you *my* friend's grown ass man and all these little hoes up here *betta* know that!" Danni keeps going.

She was getting loud and looking around, making sure everyone in the kitchen heard her. I wanted to throw a drink in her face and had to stop myself as Malone handed me the perfect weapon in a red plastic cup. He also had a drink for Danni in hand, and she hushed up briefly when he served her.

"Yea, calm all that shit down, girl," I said as she took a sip. "Mix that oil with a shot of bleach one time for the

41

streets..."

Two of Danni's AKA crew walked back in the kitchen from up front and started asking Danni something I couldn't really make out, and then KeLLy's other friend Isha walked in with her Delta sisters. The kitchen was turning into a regular danger zone and blowing my high. So I turn to Malone, "Nupe where Ricky at?"

"He out back with ole girl, I think," he tells me.

I suddenly remembered the $20 bet...and noticed that the Mona chick was nowhere in sight. Malone wasn't getting outta this one tonight – and especially if it could run me some much-needed interference at the moment.

"Nigga, where dey at?" I blurted out. "See you bullshitting bro, I want my money! Come on, walk outside with me, Nupe."

We started towards the door – for me it was more like a gimp limp. Malone stepped out first, and then my path was blocked by Isha – who stood there all of a sudden, looking up at me from her 5'3" frame.

"Y'all 'bout to leave, Rodney?" she asked, with pure innocence. "Where y'all going?"

I hesitated before answering, as out the corner of my eye I could see Malone standing behind and to the left of Isha...talking to Miss Fat Ass. Miss Fat Ass's back was facing me. It almost looked like Malone pointed back towards the door – as if Miss Fat Ass was asking where I

42

was. I coulda been tripping, but I instantly turned to my right, and was now facing Danni, who was staring me dead in the eye waiting on me to answer Isha.

"I don't know, I'm just tryna find my bruhs now."

Isha says to Danni, "Girl, it's too hot down in that basement – for real I'm ready to go."

A couple of Ques walked up to the door from the back yard to get in the house, and Isha and I moved out the way to let them pass. Isha then stepped in the house, as I stepped out into the yard. Perfect chance to limp off.

"Rodney, I got my good eye on you, Mr. Playboy!" Danni's hating ass shouts out.

I didn't acknowledge her threat and eased to the right side of the yard, where a group of niggaz were huddled in a circle...getting their freestyle on. Suddenly I didn't see Malone or Miss Fat Ass in sight – which was okay now that I was outta the clutches of KeLLy's friends...even if only for a moment.

I needed to find Ricky – and fast. I reached in my pocket for my cell phone...and found nothing but a lighter and a tube of *Carmex*.

SHIT! WHERE THE FUCK IS MY PHONE?!?!!?

I couldn't remember where I last had it, not since we were in the car smoking. I may have left it there, but then again it coulda fell somewhere in that damned basement. I started to walk back the other way through the yard quickly, ignoring the swelling starting to flare up in my right knee.

Should I walk to the car or try to go back to the basement? Where the fuck did Malone walk off to with that fat booty bitch? This is some bullshit.

I quickly decided to head back to the car and see if it was there. Worst case scenario, I might run into Ricky and then we just try to call it from his phone.

About halfway down the street, I see *Jay* the *Que* talking to two chicks – one of them a white girl I don't recognize and the other one was Mona – the chick Malone was supposed to be on.

"Kappa ass Rodney! You out, cuzz?" he calls out loudly.

"Naw I gotta find my phone, brooo!" I shake my head. "You seen Ricky, though?"

Jay stepped away from the ladies and put his arm around my shoulder. Then he stepped off to the side, near the corner and lowered his voice, "Cuzz – I'm tryna slide off somewhere. But you know these two hoes are set-out bitches..."

I looked over at Mona and the skinny white girl, "Get the fuck outta here bro!"

"Straight up!" he smiles. "I mean, I know the white

girl is. Nigga the Bras be over here running *through* her ass, cuzz! I bet the little other bitch 'a *go* too, though! Nigga stick around, don't leave!"

"I ain't leaving bro, I gotta find my ph..."

Jay walked off before I could finish and put his arm around the white chick and got in her ear. This nigga obviously could give 2 fucks about my phone right now – which was understandable. He and the white girl stepped about five feet away from the corner and kept talking.

The whole time, and it took me a second to notice it – but the Mona chick is staring me dead in the face. I shrug it off, more concerned about my phone than tryna figure out why Malone still ain't hopped on this chick – and so I start walking away towards the car at the end of the block.

Of course, Mona stops me after two steps, "Hey what's wrong, Rodney – you lost ya phone?"

How the fuck does she know my name???

"Yeah, how you know? You seen Ricky? Where ya friend at?"

"They might be still in the car," she says. "Come on – I'll walk wit you. You wanna call it from mine?"

"Oh you got a cell?" I ask, shocked. Most people didn't have cell phones in '03. "Yeah, I need to find my shit man – right on..."

She reaches in her small brownish purse and fumbles around in it, looking for her phone. A couple of pieces of chewing gum fall out and to the ground...and then some lip gloss...and then a gold condom wrapper. From a mile away and drunk as a skunk, I can tell a Magnum wrapper when I see one.

"Damn, where is my phone?" she says to herself. "Oh, here it is..."

I'm kneeling down in the street to pick up her lost items, and she finally notices what fell out.

"Ooops, my bad," she chuckles awkwardly.

"Oh, you good," I laugh it off with her, easing the embarrassment. "We grown. I ain't mad about it."

Mona takes the items out of my hand, "Well I'm mad about it. Shit."

"Why you say that?" my curiosity peaks.

She replies plainly, "Cuz, shit ain't nobody at the party trying to help me use this shit..."

I know she didn't say what I think she...

My eyebrow raises, "Use *what* shi...."

"Boy you *know* what I'm saying," she cuts me off, getting straight to the point. "I thought this was a *real* after-party. That's what I was told anyway."

Going with the flow, I asked her, "So you tryna have a '*real*' after-party, huh??"

"Hell yeah," she answered, without batting an eye. "Do you know where a real one at???"

*　　　*　　　*　　　*　　　*

7

3:18am

"Do you know where a *real* one at?" she had asked...

If this was a movie...you woulda heard that 'record scratch' sound right then. Or if I ever put this shit in a song – I would tell *Jaz* to drop the beat right when the lyric screamed, "And then she asked *'where the REAL party at?'*". If this was in the era of *texts*...I woulda had a couple of minutes to think of something clever to shoot back.

The fucked-up part about *real life/in-the-here-and-now* type moments such as these is...there's no *pause* or *rewind*, no way to run that part back. No time to think about how to react, no way to outline what happens next. You just have to live in the moment, and trip off how it all went down later.

In my mind, though – I *do* have that power to slow shit down...it's a pre-req in *The Art of Cheating*. So, in my *mind*, my reaction in the moment moved at my pace. I gathered my thoughts, assessed the situation in its entirety, and was strategic and careful about my verbiage and tone. In my mind, this whole scene moved slower.

In *reality*, however, my reaction took less than two seconds. Mona stared me dead in the eye, waiting on my reply. I stared her dead in hers...bit my lip...and said, "Where my dude Malone at? He might know where one at."

I mean, I'm not the cutthroat type of guy – I know this bitch was on my nigga Malone earlier. Plus – if Malone don't fuck the chick because I fuck her, it's almost like I'm cheating in our bet – right? I'm a cheater, but I ain't cheating my guys outta no bread. And make no mistake about it, this chick *is* trying to fuck. So, if Malone *still* don't fuck after I pass this pussy up...this nigga is most definitely giving me that dub and can't ever say anything to me in the area of fuckery like ever fuckin' again after this. So I throw the *oop*...hoping it stays in the air long enough for Malone to get the easy score.

"Shit, I don't know," she sounds fed up. "He ain't been saying shit to me. He shy or something..."

Damn. Don't shake ya head, Rod.

"But he can come, too," she continues. "I'm down with all'at shit. Where he at?"

This would be another record scratch moment...

"You say what now?" I ask in my best *Martin Lawrence* voice.

"Boy, you heard me – wassup?!" Mona doesn't flinch. "I'm tryna leave with y'all..."

"You tryna leave with me *and* Malone? Shut the fuck up!!!" I grin in disbelief.

"No, not just you and Malone," she corrects me. "I'm trying to leave with y'all *period*. The Nupes."

"Aww shit. So what choo really tryna do?" I put my game face on. "I'm a real to-the-point guy, ya dig?"

She takes a step toward me, now she's right in my face. This is the first time I had a chance to look at the bitch. She's short – 5'4" and about my complexion. I didn't notice until now the bitch had on glasses. Little nerdy looking chick. Her hair was pulled back in a ponytail…if you could call it a tail. She had on blue jeans and a striped blouse and her c-cup tits were on my chest. I remember this bitch being shy in the car, now all of a sudden, she's lifting my shirt up and reaching down in my boxers to grab my dick, "You *know* what I'm trying to do. Party."

My wooD stands up instantly, and my knees start to wobble. Ignoring the pain, I let out a long, drawn-out moan, "Daaaaaaaaaaamn......shit. What about yo friend?"

"Who, Tamm..."

I cut her off, gasping, "Naw, the lil white girl that walked off wit Ja..."

Mona keeps squeezing my dick in the middle of the street, "Yeah see, she wanna stay over here with *them Que niggas*. I wanna go with *y'all*..."

Her hand flops outta my shorts as I pull away, "Ok. Lemme go find these niggas..."

*　　*　　*　　*　　*

12:19pm

"Ok, so you said you saw them right before y'all left the party and *what* happened?" KeLLy awaits the details.

"Girl, I saw the nigga fall on the stairs and he gon try to *play* it off," Danni explains. "I'm tryna see if he ok...and he gon get smart, talmbout some *'why the fuck you acting like you care?'*"

Ana and *'unknown girl'* are laughing...but Danni is noticeably mad as she talks to KeLLy, "Girl see I don't know how you do it. Nope – couldn't be *me*! And then I think he was trying to hurry outside to talk to that one little tramp I cannot stand..."

Renée and Kells both exclaim, *"Who?!?!"*

"That one Zeta – **Leslie** - y'all know who I'm talking about!" Danni squeals. "I can't *stand* that bitch – for real!"

I almost roll over and scream, 'Who the fuck is *LESLIE*?!?!'

Cuz I sure as hell didn't know – but that was a good thing, so when I get questioned about it later, I'll be telling the truth: *'I don't know no Leslie and I have no idea what you talking about, Kells!!!'*

Instead though, I continue to lay still frowning, though none of them could see my face. I can't *stand* Danni's ass...*always tryna get some shit started!!!*

"Naw girl, I ain't see Leslie but I *did* see Tammy talking to *Ricky* in the car when I pulled up," Isha chimes in. "And I coulda *swore* I saw that bitch giving him head in the car!"

KeLLy's voice goes up a notch, "Bitch you *lying* – which Ricky?!?!"

"*KAPPA*-RICKY!!!!" Isha reveals. "I am not lying, y'all. When we rode past the car, it looked like she had jumped up – head in his lap! Bitch, I ain't crazy!!"

"Oh, I wonder if *that's* who he left with...after Rodney threw up?" KeLLy tries to piece the puzzle together.

"That shit so nasty," Danni mumbles under her breath.

KeLLy keeps pondering, "Cuz Ricky said that he left Rodney at Malone's cuz he got sick and *he* went to get some action thinking *Malone* was bringing Rodney home. I'm just *tryna make it make sense.*"

"I don't know, but I did see Ricky talking to Rodney *and* Malone in the Ques' back yard right before *we* all left," Isha remembers. "I didn't see *Tammy* nowhere around them, but I tell you who I *did* see with them..."

The whole room chimes in, even *me* this time under my liquored breath, *"WHO?!?!?"*

*　　*　　*　　*　　*

8

12:22pm

"Shhhh...girl y'all be *quiet* 'fore y'all wake him up!"
KeLLy whispers, hushing everyone up. Then to Isha,
"Who bitch?!?"

"Yeah shit, I wanna know who too now my *damn*
self," Ana says.

Now they've all lowered their voices...thinking I'm
still sleep. "Girl naw, not like y'all thinking, I'm talmbout I
saw them all talking to *Jay*," Isha clarifies.

"Que Jay?" Danni doesn't quite understand.
"*And...?*"

"Y'all remember Ricky and Jay was fonking *hard*
when Ricky first transferred up here last year," Isha
explains.

KeLLy sounds disappointed, "Awww bitch you *late*,
they *been* squashed that shit."

"Yeah, you know the Kappas & Ques always been
tight on this campus," Danni adds.

Isha is offended, "Duh bitch I know *that*. Well, hell I didn't know Ricky & Jay squashed that shit. Ricky ain't even pledge at *this* school – how was I supposed to know? Y'all can kiss my ass!!!"

Renée offers her input, "Isha girl don't worry 'bout them! You graduated last year – you ain't got time to be coming down here getting in all this little childish mess. And I know you don't even talk to Jay like that no more."

"I know, right?" Isha turns to Renée. "Thank you, girl!"

"Oh, stop *jeffin*..." Danni yells out, like the true asshole she is.

KeLLy was cracking up, "Right...Danni bitch you *stupid!!* What was they talking about though Isha?"

"Who? Aww, Ricky and Jay and 'nem?" Isha gets back to the story. "Oh I couldn't hear them, we left. That's when everybody started leaving cuz they ain't have no *air* in the damn basement and it was hot as hell in that house..."

"Aww ok. So where did everybody go after that?" Kells had to know.

*　　*　　*　　*　　*

3:26am

Ricky was standing near the back door to the house, listening to the rap freestyle session when I finally found him. The party had died down and most of the crowd was walking to their cars, but there were a few folks staying behind...mostly Ques.

"Nupe, we gotta *roll!!!* Got it popping!" I tell Ricky.

"Hold up...hol'up," Ricky waves me off, bobbing his head to the rapping.

"*NIGGA*, no! We gotta *go*," I put more urgency behind my words.

"Nigga where you *been?*" Ricky wonders. "I heard you fell down the stairs and shit...

"Bro fuck that – *listen* to me..."

I grab him by the elbow and explain to him the situation. We need to shake the spot now, while I got this bitch hot and horny...and never look back. I'm so caught up in the shit that Ricky has to remind me that he originally was on the little bitch's friend, "Nigga I just got some head in the car from the lil' bitch friend. I'm suppose to go to breakfast in the morning with the *Zeta* chick bro!!!"

"Nigga, still go take dat bitch to breakfast, but right now – we need to take *this* bitch back to Malone's crib and

59

beat the *brakes* off her ass!!" I advise him. "Fuck that shit
for real!!!"

Ricky laughs, "Nigga you *them*! Bro that little Mona
bitch not fucking wit me after I been on her partner all
night!!"

"Bro look, I'm not bullshitting you – this lil' bitch
tryna get ran," I keep explaining. "By the Nupes. Nigga we
need to call Paul & Lil Tony and see if they wanna come
through, too."

Ricky started to think about it, "Naw nigga it's after 3,
going on 4 in a minute. Dem niggas ain't up."

He's right, I decide as I look over my shoulder, "Man
well fuck it, we just need the keys to Malone spot then..."

"Nigga *I* got his keys – I drove!!!"

"Bro, we can go *now* – dis bitch just went to go tell da
white girl she got a ride home," I stated with anxiousness.

"Yeah, cuz Tammy been left nigga! That's what I'm
saying yo – you tryna fuck *my* shit up with that lil bitch
Rod!" Ricky suspects, weighing the risks.

"Bro, I don't even think Tammy know dis bitch is *like*
that…she told me not to say nothing to Tammy right
when I walked off to find you. I'a still holla at Tammy,
bro if I was you…but *fuck* all'at shit right now, nigga!
Come on – let's be out!

"Well shit, we can't leave *Malone*, Nupe," Ricky points out.

And he's right, yet again. My head drops with impatience, "Man, *fuck*...where is this nigga at?! He walked off with this other little bitch I was on earlier. I should leave that nigga."

We start walking around to the front of the house and Ricky laughs, "Nigga how you gon leave that nigga and I got the keys???"

"You know I'm just talking shit," I tell him, trying to sound serious. "I'm just saying we need to go – Malone ain't getting no pussy no way. Where *is* this nigga, man?"

Ricky points up ahead, "Here this guy is right here..."

Malone is in the front of the Que house, standing at the foot of the steps as more folks are walking to their cars. I'm still drunk and high, though I have sobered up just enough to get on my one-two. My walk is still limp from my knee sprain, and my movements are delayed.

But I'm coherent enough to hear what's going on...and at that moment, Malone was standing at the foot of the steps, telling people to come through his crib for the 'after-after party'...

Wow! What is this nigga doing?!?!?!

Ricky gets to him before I can and puts the bug in his ear before they both walk back in my direction on the side of the house. Ricky has to literally walk Malone by the back of his neck to get him to calm down about how dope the after-after party 'bout to be.

"Yo, let's get the fuck outta here, bro," I start walking towards the car once they get close.

"Hold up, this guy got folks thinking the Nupes having a set at his spot," Ricky lets me know.

"Yeah, man why you do that shit before you talked to the bruhs?" I'm sick of his shit. "You's a retarded dude boa. And did you fuck that big booty bitch you was talking to, nigga?"

We kept walking to the next block where we parked, and I could see Mona walking up ahead, to meet us at the whip.

"What big booty bitch?" Malone asks me. "Nigga I got two dymes' phone numbers tonight! I only fuck dymes!!!"

"What I just tell you, Phi? The most *non-pussy-gettin-ass-nigga!!!*" I glance at Ricky, before telling Malone, "Boy you owe me twice for this…"

"Nigga, please," Malone retorts.

Ricky gets frustrated, "Y'all niggaz quit fussing like some hoes and come on! We gotta figure out how to stop this *after-after party* crowd from showing up!!"

"Nigga, how many muhfuckaz you tell that shit?!" I

snarl at Malone.

Just then, Jay the Que suddenly called my name from the side of the house...towards the backyard. I mean, the nigga is literally yelling, super hyphy like it's an emergency, "Aye Rod!!!! Hold up...y'all niggaz can't leave! I need to holla at *all* you Kappa niggaz *RIGHT NOW!!!*"

Gotdamn man! What now???

*   *   *   *   *

9

3:34am

Ricky looks up, and immediately gets defensive, "Damn...now what this hoe ass nigga want?"

"Chill out, Nupe," I stopped him, trying to keep the peace.

"I'm good, bro...dat old shit dead," Ricky reassures me. *"I'm just saying..."*

We start walking back towards the house to meet Jay on the west side. He's grinning from ear-to-ear, as usual, "Party at the *Nupes* crib huh?!?! Aye man, how long y'all gon be over there? Walk back here with me, lemme holla at y'all niggaz..."

"Naw cuzz, for real we ain't even tryna do no party at the spot – we tryna get on some otha," I hinted.

So now we all standing in the Que's back yard again – just us now. The yard has been cleared and there's no music playing, so we're all speaking lowly. Jay tells us how the Ques have a couple setouts in the crib and they was gonna stop by our set after they did their thing. Now that he knows we're not really having the party, he invites us to

65

hang around if we want. No thanks – we good.

Our little guy talk gets interrupted by some cars honking as they rode by – looks like *Isha* with some other Deltas. Jay yells out something at Isha and they drive off as he laughs with us about how he used to bang Isha's back in and now she's mad cuz he ain't all in her face.

We all dap up and Jay starts towards the back door, when suddenly he says, "Oh I see what *y'all* niggas on! Aye do that shit ole *Kappa* ass niggas!"

We look to the right at what he's referring to and there is *Mona*...standing outside the gate...waiting on us. She smiles at us, and then to Jay, "Shut the fuck up Jay, y'all know I don't like folks knowing my busines..."

I grab her by the waist and start pacing, "Come on, let's get to the fuckin' car...."

*   *   *   *   *

1:40pm

"Did y'all end up stopping over Malone's?" KeLLy asked her girls.

"Naw I don't think anybody went over there," Danni said. "I heard nobody showed up, they didn't even have no music playing when *Shonda* and 'nem rode past. I mean, it was almost *3:30* by then, girl."

"Right, it was time to go home," Isha co-signed, with her jeffin' ass.

"Bitch, you wasn't trying to go home...I know better," KeLLy calls her out.

Isha stands her ground, "Girl I got something to eat and went right over my sorors' and went to sleep. Don't even play."

"Well, I was just hoping *somebody* got some dick last night since I *clearly* didn't," Kells takes a shot at me. I could almost feel her staring at the back of my head.

Renée starts shouting, "KeLLy shut up, girl...you are too much!"

"Y'all, speaking of food – can we go get something to eat?" Isha interjects. "Y'all ain't hungry?"

"Me and Renée ate on the way down here," Ana tells them.

"Come on, cuz we gotta get some more liquor anyway," Isha hops up. "KeLLy, y'all we 'a be back...y'all need anything?"

"Bring back some ice," Kells requests.

"Danni, you driving? I gotta let you out," Isha says

to the sound of her car keys dangling.

I can hear the door opening, and feel them stepping over me, and then there's the sound of cars starting, a few laughs, and then the door closes. KeLLy steps over me but walks up towards my upper body and kneels in…shaking me by my shoulder, "Rodney!!! Are you still sleep?? Wake up!"

*   *   *   *   *

3:39am

So Ricky is driving of course. Same seating arrangement as before, only this time Malone and I have switched and I'm behind Ricky. Mona is in the back with me, after making a comment that she needs me to sit next to her this time since '*last time Malone act like he was scared to touch her*'. Ricky and I are discussing how to end the party Malone publicized before it starts…

"Nigga, we can just tell muhfuckaz it's over soon as we get there," I suggested.

"Naw bro, we can't do that," Ricky disagreed. "Ain't no telling who gon show up and we can't get out the car with her, while telling folks the party *over…*"

"Yea, I guess you right," I decided, as my mind

started drifting.

Mona has her hand on my right leg…and she takes mine and puts it on her belt buckle. I follow suit and start to undo her pants.

"We can just have a few folks over, y'all," Malone is still campaigning for the party. "Get on some bones or spades…"

"Nigga!!!" I shouted at him. "It's *3:30* in the muhfuckin' morning…ain't nobody tryna play no spades and dominoes, fool!!!"

Mona lifts up to pull her pants down just enough for me to rub her pussy through her cotton panties. Her lips are like unusually fat…you can see the camel toe and clit poking through the garments. "Damn, yo pussy fat," I whispered.

"It's wet, too," she whispers, but not as low as I did.

"Damn, y'all fuckers getting the party started already," Ricky says, looking at us through the rearview mirror.

"Naw, but listen…for real," I glance at the dashboard. "It's going on 4 o'clock."

Ricky nods his head, "Yeah, that's real spit – it's late as a muhfucka. People might not even show up."

Mona has pulled her panties to the side and tells me

to stick a finger in. Just one finger…cuz two will be too much and she wants to be opened up when we fuck her. Her pussy is suuuuuper wet…a small pocket of wetness is sitting where her pussy and ass cheeks meet. She tells me to go slow.

"Nigga, if not that many people show up, we should be ok!" I said to Rick.

"What you mean?" he asked. "We just get down out in the open cuz it ain't that many folks??? Rod, you still drunk!!!"

"Bro, I ain't even drunk…hear me out," I pleaded. "This what I'm sayi…."

My words fade out as Mona has suddenly stopped me from fingering her….and she sits up and leans over toward me, frantically trying to unzip my shorts. "Pull ya dick out," she says. Not low or whispering at all.

Ricky swerves the car, losing composure momentarily, "Damn, lil mama, you not fucking around back there, I see…"

"Y'all," Mona mutters. "…y'all gotta forgive me but I always wanted to fuck some *Kappas*. And I ain't had no dick in over a year."

My eyes widened, "Whoa…are you serious??"

"Yeah right, you know you be getting it in out here," Ricky doesn't believe her for a second. "Bitch, don't lie."

"Naw, I ain't fucked since I broke up with my man last year," Mona insists. "I love giving head, so I been doing dat, but I ain't had no dick. I'm serious."

"Here…have some now," I point my hardness at her. "Get this muhfucka wet."

Mona doesn't hesitate…and opens her mouth wide to take my whole dick down to her throat. I can feel her lips touching my pelvis and she's kissing my balls with her bottom lip. My shit throbs in her throat and I grab the back of her neck, trying to force her even deeper. She gags and comes up for air…then repeats that sequence. You can hear her slurping loudly.

"Damn…save some of that shit for me, nigga," Ricky feels left out.

Mona comes up for air and tells him, "Don't worry, I got you. And I bet I suck yo dick better than that bitch Tammy…"

"Damn, I thought that was ya homie," my jaw dropped.

Mona sucks my head and pops it back out her mouth. "It is, but she know she can't suck no mean one like me! I ain't gon say shit though Pretty Ricky, I ain't no hater! *Trust!!!*"

"I can dig it," Ricky's face lights up. "Yeah, see I like this chick, Rod!"

71

She keeps taking dick to the head while we ride. She's got my shit sloppy wet and jacking it with her right hand. Her hands are small and soft, and she's working it like a champ. I've got my right hand down her jeans and palming her ass cheek…it has a nice roundness to it that wasn't noticeable before.

"Bro, this nigga Malone up here *knocked* out," Ricky bursts out laughing.

"I'm not surprised," I throw my head back, enjoying the throat hugs.

"Bro, y'all hold tight, we pulling up," Ricky gives a heads up. "Looks like its two cars here…"

I look out the window, Mona still sucking my meat sloppily in my lap. Ricky is right, there are two cars outside Malone's crib, parked in the gravel lot to the side. I pull Mona up by her skeet ponytail and we both start to fasten our pants.

"Aight, we gotta figure out how to shake these muhfuckaz," Ricky said as he started to circle around the lot.

"Bro, who is that in that white car?" I shouted, looking to my right. "Looks like some *Zetas* standing behind it???"

"It *issss* some Zetas!!!" Ricky noticed. "Yup – sholl look like it..."

My eyes widen and I yell – not loud, but loud
enough to wake Malone up and get everyone's attention,
"Ohhhhhhh shit….is that *ZETA Tammy* right there with
them, bro?!?!?!?"

*   *   *   *   *

10

3:45am

Ricky's head snaps to the right and he swerves the car to the left trying to get a look, "*Where?!?!?!*"

Mona and I start laughing hysterically and I tell my nigga, "Naaaaw…I'm just playing, bro. That's them Zetas from KC, I think."

"You bitch ass nigga…quit playing so muthafuckin' much, nigga!" Ricky snapped. "Almost made me crash!"

"Into what bro?" I'm cackling. "Ain't nothing out here to run into! That shit was funny, yo…"

Ricky doesn't think so, "Fuck y'all, I'm ready to get some pussy around this muhfucka! Malone, wake yo drunk ass up! You got some condoms in this bitch?"

"Damn, you know I don't keep dem muhfuckaz," I suddenly realized I didn't have any hats.

"I got two," Mona said.

"That ain't enuff," Ricky shakes his head. "Malone – wake yo ass up, bro! We at yo party, lil nigga…"

"Nupe, you got some rubbers in the crib?" I asked the sleepyhead, knowing he probably didn't.

"Nope…I don't think so," he mumbles.

"I don't even know why I asked you that…why would you???"

"Aww nigga, I just stop and get em when I'm 'bout to get it in," Malone shot back. "Y'all niggaz always talking shit!!!"

"Nigga whatever – you prolly don't even know how to put one on, nigga," I keep swinging with the verbal jabs.

"Why y'all clowning Malone?" Mona comes to his defense. "Leave my boo alone…"

"Fuck that lil crazy nigga," I frowned.

Ricky put the car in park and brought us back down to earth, "Listen you muhfuckaz – we need to go get some condoms. One of us need to stay and tell people the party is a wrap."

"Good idea," I agreed. "Malone, you and Mona go in…tell them it's a wrap and we'll go to the store and grab some hats. Ain't nobody gonna think you fucking her, anyway."

"Fuck you, Rod," Malone said, clearly tired of my mouth.

The plan is set, and we quickly hop out the car to fall in line. The Zetas ask where everybody is as soon as I open the back door and just as swift, they get in their car and pull off once they realize me and Ricky are leaving. I get in the front seat, and soon as I sit down, I feel my phone underneath me. Talk about a lucky night. I forgot all about that muhfuckin' phone.

Mona and Malone start towards the back porch – that's the only way that Malone enters the building since his front door is blocked off with all types of junk. By the time Ricky and I make a circle in the gravel and turn around...the other car of guests is driving away as well. It'll take us 15 or 20 minutes to get back from the gas station so by that time...any latecomers would obviously see that everything was shut down and we should have Malone's spot to ourselves.

4:02am

Rick flies to the store and back...and it actually took us about 12 minutes round trip. Our biggest fear was that Malone would somehow fuck up the whole deal while we were gone, and we cursed at each other for having the bright idea to leave the bitch with *him*, of all people. Once we pulled back up, the lot was empty and all of the lights in the house were off.

"Damn, Malone already done set it off, bro!" Ricky scolds me. "See, y'all be talking that *shit*..."

I wasn't the least bit convinced. Taking the keys from Ricky, I opened the back door and hit the light to find

Mona on the couch to the right (*the living room was in the back of the place*). She was lying to the far end against the arm and watching some infomercial on the 20-inch tv in front of her. Malone was sitting in the love seat by the wall on the left...knocked the fuck out. That seemed about right.

Ricky heads towards the restroom down the hall to the far right as I turn the light back off and sit on the couch next to Mona, pulling a *Red Bull* and the 12-pack of condoms out the store bag. The condom box falls to the floor in front of me. I reach across Mona to the desk lamp and flick the switch, illuminating the room with red light. So now there's just enough light in the room...not too dark, not too bright.

"That nigga went right to sleep, didn't he?" I asked her, already knowing the answer.

"Yeah, I told him I had a condom and he was like, '*wait 'til the bruhs get back*'," Mona confirms. "So yea, whatever. Cum'ere..."

She scoots closer and reaches for my zipper, but I stop her, "Naw, take them clothes off..."

She stands up without hesitation and pulls her blouse over her head. I notice she has a tattoo circling her pierced navel and her stomach is actually flat...which was a shocker. The bitch looked kinda chubby in the blouse earlier. Not now. Her 34C's were damn nearly falling out her pink bra, which only stayed on for three more seconds. She stared me in the eye as she unbuttoned her jeans, sliding them to the ground and off her legs…one at a time. Her purplish panties stayed put…but there was a huge wet spot in the front telling the story of her anticipation. This little freak bitch had been waiting all night to get fucked.

I undid my *Dockers* shorts and slid them to my knees, pulling my dick through my boxers. Mona sat back down and started stroking me slowly…spitting on her hands.

"You know I been wanting to fuck you for a minute," she says.

Reaching over to rub her nipples, I replied, "Naw, I ain't even know you existed to know you was checking for me. I thought you just wanted to fuck some *Nupes*. Now you always wanted to fuck *me*?"

"I mean yeah…both," she explained. "Me and my cousin used to talk about you when she was messing with one of your bruhs last year…"

"Who is yo cousin?" I wondered.

"She used to mess with yo one dark-skinned bruh," she gets more detailed. "I can't remem…"

"It don't e'en matter," I interrupted. "*Here*.…"

I thrusted upward, pushing her head down until her mouth met my **HoLLyWooD** again and then I rested onto the couch, holding the back of her neck and humping her throat until she gagged. She comes up with teary eyes and takes a long exhale. My dick is jumping in my lap. "Come on, freak," I guide her head back down, taking a fistful of her hair, which has now come loose. She gets up on the couch, ass in the air to my right.

Ricky comes out of the restroom and walks past us, into the kitchen. I can hear him making a drink. To my left, Malone is now snoring.

I continue to fuck her face, controlling her head bobs by pulling and releasing her strands of hair...and she's moaning with pleasure at this. I let go of her head to slap her ass cheeks – hard as fuck – trying to put my print in dem muhfuckas. She moans with the impact.

"Take them panties off, girl," I demanded.

I yank at her panties and she works them down her legs with her left hand, leaning her body against me and the couch to keep her balance with my dick in her mouth. She's slurping loud and sucking hard...speeding up her pace...and I pull her closer to me by her ass, reaching around her cheek to touch her pussy. She's dripping wet. I mean, literally...*dripping* wet. It's running down her legs.

Ricky walks in and stands in front of her elevated ass, and just looks at the bitch for a minute – sipping his drink. "Damn, she got a nice little ass, huh?"

"Maaan. Pussy fat too, nigga," I tell him.

"Lemme see," Ricky sits down on the other end, putting his drink next to the lamp on the table. He starts playing with her pussy…and Mona likes this shit. I can tell because now she's making *herself* gag on my dick…and not coming up for air.

"Damn, girl yo shit back here clenching up," Ricky whispered lowly. "I like that shit. Damn…"

She moans again, in heaven. This is like a dream come true for this young lady. She's the center of attention for some player ass Nupes. It's quite understandable. And now I wanna fuck.

So I stand up, pushing her towards Ricky, as my shorts drop to the floor. Then I walk a few steps away from the couch, tearing open the condom box, "Suck my nigga off, bitch…"

"Can this muhfucka suck some dick bro?" Ricky looks my way.

"Yeah. She right, bruh…"

Mona stands up too, and helps Ricky get out of his jeans….as he moves over to where I was sitting before. Mona then drops to her knees and takes Ricky in her mouth…bobbing her head fast and moaning in a high pitch.

I squeeze her ass check hard, digging my nails in it – and lift upward, "Girl, get that ass in the air! Quit acting like that…"

Mona pulled her head out of Ricky's lap, who had

81

both hands up and behind his head now…in that player stance.

"Damn, y'all niggas treating me like a slut n'shit," Mona takes in the scene.

Ricky and I just smirked, before replying in unison, *"CUZ YOU ARE!!!"*

*　　*　　*　　*　　*

11

4:20am

I drop to my knees behind her, and she starts sucking Ricky with no hands...spreading both ass cheeks for me. Her pussy literally got juices running everywhere and as I start to slide in – it's throbbing nonstop. She moans in a much lower tone this time, but louder.

So now I'm going to work...and I mean, I'm pounding this shit. Ricky got a grip on the hoe's head with both hands, stroking her throat like a madman...and I'm on one knee and one foot – gripping her waist with both hands. She's throwing it back in rhythm. But every few strokes, Malone's snoring gets loud and annoying. After 'bout 45 seconds...I can't take it anymore.

Still thrusting, I yell over at Malone, "Aye MALONE! Wake yo ass up nigga and get some of dis pussy!!!"

He doesn't respond at all, still snoring. I spot this empty red cup near my foot on the floor and I somehow manage to keep humping and pick it up, lunging it at Malone in the corner behind me. It taps his nose before landing in his lap.

"*NUPE*! Wake the fuck up, boy!" I screamed at him.

This time he comes to, eyes opening slowly. I turn away from him to keep fucking, now that I know he's up.

"Ok, ok, ok," he mumbles. "Alright!"

Mona is bent over and squatting still now, letting me deep stroke it while she continues to spread her cheeks. Her pussy gripping me hard as *fuck*. The build-up is intense, and my hearing goes dead for the split second before I let loose. I can't hear my grunts, but I know dey there. I keep thrusting and pumping, smacking her ass as I slow down to finish my nut.

She keeps giving Ricky dome after I pull out. When I stand up, I notice Malone ain't in the chair no more. Maybe he went to the kitchen. I headed to the restroom to clean up so I ain't really sure about that part. Even down the hall, though, I can still hear Mona slurping on Ricky.

"Damn dat bitch ain't playing no games!" I mumbled as I washed up in the sink.

By the time I come out the restroom, Malone is sitting back in the chair now, eating some fuckin' *Doritos*. I reach for my boxers, face screwed up, "Bro, what are you doing?"

Ricky is taking his pants off and Mona is standing in the middle of the floor, rubbing her pussy. I'm sick of this shit.

86

"Aye, suck his dick, Mona Lisa," I motion for her to hook my lil bro up.

She immediately heads toward Malone and drops to her knees, tugging at his belt. Ricky is standing up with condom in hand and I sit back on the big couch, getting dressed.

"Pull it out, boy. Come on," she tells Malone, taking control.

"Nigga, act like you know what to do with some pussy," I bit my lip.

Malone ignores me, and looks Mona in the eye, "You ready? It's *BIG*..."

He then gives a slight chuckle as she reaches in his boxers to help him get free. "Well *damn*," she gasps at the sight of his member before quickly slurping loudly on it.

Ricky walks up behind her and lowers down to get settled in. Malone then suddenly stands up and thrusts hard into Mona's mouth...choking the bitch into a violent cough, "Come on! Suck it!"

He then turns into a crazy beast, standing up and fucking her mouth like it's pussy, as Ricky starts smashing into her from the back. I figure this is a good time for a drink, and so I step into the kitchen. Mona is moaning loud as fuck now, telling Ricky to fuck her harder in between Malone's mouth pumps.

After about ten minutes or so, Ricky finishes and gets dressed, while Malone takes Mona to the couch. She lays back with her legs in the air, and Malone lowers down into her gaping pussy, pounding hard like a madman. This nigga Malone is like for real going *in* on this little bitch. It's like he taking out years of frustration and struggle out on her ass. Ricky comes in the kitchen, and we laugh at how hard Malone is going while I roll another blunt.

It was about **4:56** when stepped out on the back porch to smoke. Malone is *still* fucking this chick twenty minutes later when we come back in. Now he done crawled on top and started slow stroking. If this is for real the first time he's had pussy in a while, my nigga is treating it like it might be his last time ever. Ricky and I stand there talking shit for a minute while Malone pulls her hair and goes even harder. It's funny, but I need this nigga to hurry up, though.

Before I know it, now it's **5:30am**…and reality is starting to sink in. I done been out *all night*, getting fucked up, and fucking. I gotta figure out how to sneak my ass back in the house with KeLLy blowing a fuse.

Ricky and I post up in the kitchen to start weighing my options. "Bro…this nigga is *still* fucking," he shakes his head at the sounds from the other room.

I give a slight chuckle, "Man I told you dat nigga ain't had no pussy in forever."

"So, what's the play? How we gon do this?" Ricky's tone gets serious.

"Ok, so I'm thinking…I might have an idea," I spark up what was left of the Swisher. "This nigga need to hurry up, though."

"I know, I'm hungry as a muhfucka yo," Ricky licks his lips. "Oh *shit*! I'm supposed to take the little Zeta bitch to breakfast at 8! Aye MALONE – come on bro!!!"

Malone finally busts a nut, and stumbles into the bathroom. I lean in the living room to talk to Mona as she gathers her shit, waiting on Malone to come out.

"Aye you good?"

"Yeah, I'm gravy," Mona smiles in satisfaction. "My pussy sore as fuck, though! Damn nigga!"

I put my fist out to dap her, cuz that's how her pussy *should* feel, "Aye, but you found yo *'real party'*, though!"

"Ok!! Straight VIP nigga. For real!"

*   *   *   *   *

6:07am

So now we all in the car again, Malone in the back with her – me and Rick up front. The sun is coming up. I can hear birds chirping n'shit. Mona tells us to hang a left on *Russell*, and we pull up at her cousin's crib. She hops out without speaking and we ride off before she hits the porch.

"Ok, so what we supposed to use for fake throw-up?" Ricky starts going over the plan again.

"Bro *I* say I should make myself throw up *for real*…wipe that shit right on my shirt. Make it hella authentic," I check to make sure the zipper on my shorts ain't still open.

Malone laughs from the back seat, "Bro, that shit is not gonna work! You a fool, Rod!!!"

"Y'all look – I'm telling you – dis shit is foolproof," I said with devious certainty. "All y'all gotta do is get me in the door, lay me on the floor. Tell her how fucked up we got last night, and get the fuck up outta der. She gon leave me on the floor, and I'ma lay right there until it's safe."

"Bro, but how you gon know when it's safe?" Ricky was still skeptical. "Nigga, how long are you willing to lay on the floor – faking drunk and playing hangover?

"*Nigga*! As long as I *have* to," I tell him. "Y'all think I'm playing. Come on, pull over up here. I'm finna make myself hurl…"

*   *   *   *   *

2:43pm

"Rodney!!! Get up boy!" KeLLy yells at me again, jolting out of my sleep. "Get these nasty ass clothes off!! Go take a shower so you can lay in the bed…"

My eyes open slowly, and I see her standing over me, mad as hell. I close my eyes quickly, moaning. Now was my chance...

"My head *huuuurt*," I whimpered.

"Well, get up! You shoulda thought about that before you did all that damn drinking," KeLLy fusses.

Renée chimed in, "Yeah Rodney, so that's what we do now? We mixing dark and light? You's a brave one…but a drunk ain't shit, I tell ya."

"I'm not playing, Rodney!" KeLLy screams with fury. "Get up – before Danni and 'nem get back! Embarrassing me, this don't make *no* damn sense!"

I manage to prop myself up on my left elbow and sit still – trying to look like I'm gathering my thoughts as I'm waking up, "What time is it?"

"It's almost **3 o'clock** boy, you been on that floor going on *9 hours!!* Dead to the world!" her voice is laced with irritation.

"Maaan," I sighed. "What the fuck?!"

"Get *UP* Rodney!" KeLLy snaps.

"How the fuck I get home? What the fuck man?"

I get on all fours and try to take a knee…and almost immediately lose my balance…to look like I'm still kinda outta it. KeLLy lets out a long sigh of frustration and helps me up. I limp down the hall and to the bathroom, moving extra slow. Her fussing from the living room drowns out as I turn the shower knob.

Before I step into the shower, I take one last look in the mirror and smile, realizing I'm finally scot-free.

On the inside, I'm laughing hysterically at everybody who *really* thought I was hungover and incoherent. On the outside, I still look the part. The cottonmouth, the liquor and vomit on my breath, the slobber stains on my face. Using the truth to your advantage is key in the *Art of Cheating*, and it's something I learned early on. Half-truths never hurt anybody. And what Kells don't know…can never, ever truly hurt her. In the end, it's just all part of the game…right?

"Last night was mad real..."

Indeed, it was HoLLy. Indeed it fuckin' was...

FIN.
(Until We Cheat Again)

ABOUT THE AUTHOR

"HoLLyRod" – the author & creator of the highly controversial and raunchy storyline, *The Art of Cheating* – is the alter-ego and pseudonym for established writer Rodney L. Henderson Jr.

Since graduating with a Business Administration degree in Computer Information Systems from the *University of Central Missouri*, Henderson has showcased his writing skills in various forms of art – including radio commercials & music, as well as poetry & promo spots for fashion companies such as *DymeWear Inc* & *Ridikulus Kouture LLC*.

HoLLyRod's short story mini-series titled ***The Art of Cheating Episodes*** introduces readers to the many characters & mystery behind **HoLLyWorld** and *The Art of Cheating*, while chronicling the ups & downs of infidelity through experiences based on real life. The ongoing series has been re-released in a special Extended Author's Cut Edition.

AVAILABLE IN eBOOK & PAPERBACK FORMATS!!!
AUDIO BOOKS COMING SOON!!!

Henderson currently resides in his home state of Missouri and spends most of his time managing & writing for *Angela Marie Publishing, LLC* – a company named after his late mother.

The Art of Cheating Episodes is published under *Lurodica Stories*, an erotica division of the publishing company.

"I just want to continue to be inspired at the notion of making her proud and keep my promise to share my talents with the world."

www.HoLLyRods.com
www.facebook.com/TheArtOfCheating
www.twitter.com/TheCheatGods

Next up on
The Art of Cheating…

SEASON 1 – EPISODE 3:
HoLLy BeLLigerence

This third flashback in *The Art of Cheating Episodes* is a tale about the boldness of the ~~beast~~ within. Following his father's and grandfather's legacies, the young playboy *HoLLyRod* is now fully immersed in the music entertainer lifestyle – and all of the *belligerence* that comes along with it. Technically in between relationships and out for blood, he meets the local model *Luscious Lisa* – who has one of the fattest asses he's ever laid eyes on through his **HoLLyShades**. After he discovers Lisa is more of a challenge than he signed up for, the career cheater has to quickly decide if older sibling temptations are worth the risks of being *HoLLyBeLLigerent*.

EXTENDED AUTHOR'S CUT EDITION
AVAILABLE NOW

Also by HoLLyRod

The Art of Cheating Episodes
(Extended Author's Cut Edition)

SEASON 1
Episode 1 - Sassy
Episode 2 - Hangover
Episode 3 - HoLLy BeLLigerence
Episode 4 - KeLLy's Revenge
Episode 5 - The HooKup
Episode 6 - Ménages

SEASON 2
Episode 1 - Cyber Pimpin' (**12/22/22**)
Episode 2 - Campus Record (**2/15/23**)
Episode 3 - A Date with Karma (**4/20/23**)
Episode 4 - The Wedding Party (**6/19/23**)
Episode 5 - HoLLy & Sug (**8/23/23**)

SEASON 3
(Spring 2024)

Angela Marie Publishing
Presents

WDFFIL EP1: Facing the Music

The OFFICIAL Soundtrack to The Art of Cheating Episodes

AVAILABLE ON ALL MUSIC PLATFORMS

DOWNLOAD OR STREAM NOW!!!!

https://distrokid.com/hyperfollow/hollyrod/wdffil-ep1-facing-the-music-4

Made in the USA
Columbia, SC
16 July 2022

63535678R00063